The story of Shelby:

The Well Behaved Dog

With Prince & Shadow

Beth Phillips

To order additional copies of this book, contact:
Xlibris
844-714-8691
www.Xlibris.com
Orders@Xlibris.com

ISBN: Softcover   978-1-6698-1466-5
        EBook   978-1-6698-1465-8

Print information available on the last page

Rev. date: 03/10/2022

This book belongs to:

~~~~~~~~~~~~~~~~~~~~~~~~~~~~~~~~~~~~~~~

Grateful acknowledgements to
Puppy Nina and Paradise Jake her parents,
Davis Island dog beach, Fort DeSoto, Petco, Ketch.

2001- I first see Shelby at All about Puppies. Peter meets me there after work to see if it is Gods will that we adopt her. Sure enough she is still there. We bring her home. Shelby loves to sit in the sliding glass door opening. Peter takes them for a walk. every morning at 5am. (illustration). Brutus and Shelby. Shelby was named after an RV friend of my parents. I always told Shelby her parents name because I didnt know mine and wanted her to know hers.

Shortly after the following July 2002 Shelby gets a new friend. A golden retreiver named Prince. Because I was working teaching during the week and tutoring at night they spent most of their days hanging around the house. When the weekends came we went to dog parks and the causeway. They had fun swimming in the water off the causeway. Sometimes they were so tired they would fall asleep on the way home.

Shelby did her dog training at Petco. She had to pass several tests including the separation anxiety test. She did great!!!

Shelby was a well behaved dog and went outside to the bathroom right away.

In 2006 it was pointed out to me that Shelby could sense illness in a person. If someone had a cut or a sore she would minister to that said person by licking the wound.

In 2013 I noticed she was also attracted to dead things in streets on walks. She would urinate on them.

Prince loved to run over to the neighbor's house before walks. He loved to roll around on his back on walks in the grass.

In 2014 Prince and I started playing hide and seek.

Prince was the new one to the pack in the neighborhood. We trained him with little hot dog pieces to walk up the sidewalk.

Halloween that year Shelby was dressed as Raggedy Ann and Prince as Zorro. Prince tore his costume off before we got to the contest.

In 2012 Prince became a therapy dog for the Humane Society pet a pet program and later the Canines for Christ dog therapy. Prince and I visited the Carrollwood Care Center and one resident was quite fond of him while another resident was not fond of him at all and the nurse on duty defended him. The resident that was fond of him would give him treats and once he vomited.

Weekends were spent at Fort DeSoto. Prince loved to run up the beach and chase the birds.

Prince and Shelby soon began to go to the Ketch daycare when I was working. I would drive miles west to drop them off and then drive miles east to work and then back again to pick them up.

They spent long hours at the West Park dog park. I would make them walk with me around the perimeter.

Their first dog grooming was at Petco. Peter got mad that Shelby's hair was cut so short. He thought it looked stupid.

Prince would accompany us to Grill smith and they even had a doggie menu.

In 2010 I brought home Shadow who completed the trio. Peter didn't want another dog but quickly grew to like Shadow. Shadow had a behavioral issue at first of taking food off the table. This was quickly corrected with a little training. Shadow then went to dog school at a dog training club. He could scale a 6-foot wall. He was excellent at the obstacle course and ran through it with no problems. Later he was trained by Robin of good dog behavior using slides to teach him confidence at Lake Park. Later shortly he was trained on a few other behavioral issues. Shadow then was interviewed for the Canines for Christ program. He received credentials but never participated much in that program.

Weekends changed in 2014 as I was working and playing music.

Shadow loves to go to the new dog park and regularly spent his Tuesdays and birthdays at the Central Bark.

Shelby and Prince first dog grooming: Peter said " Why did you get her hair cut so short. It looks stupid.

Shelby and Prince became friends with Link and Toby and were invited to their house for swimming. Shelby sat on the steps and Prince swam to the end of the pool and sat and rested and then swam back.

Shelby did not get a short haircut after that one time.

Shelby liked to sleep right next to you. Prince liked to sleep on the floor.

Prince went to the dog grooming school to be groomed. He did not tolerate the procedure well in terms of standing for a long time.

Shelby always came out to greet people. For the most part they lived in the same house with one short move over to the Forest Hills area.

Prince loved to lay on the leather couch on his back.

Shelby also learned how to do sheep herding.

At one point we had a tick population take up residence in our house which required a vet trip to remove the ticks and housing until the tick problem could be rectified.

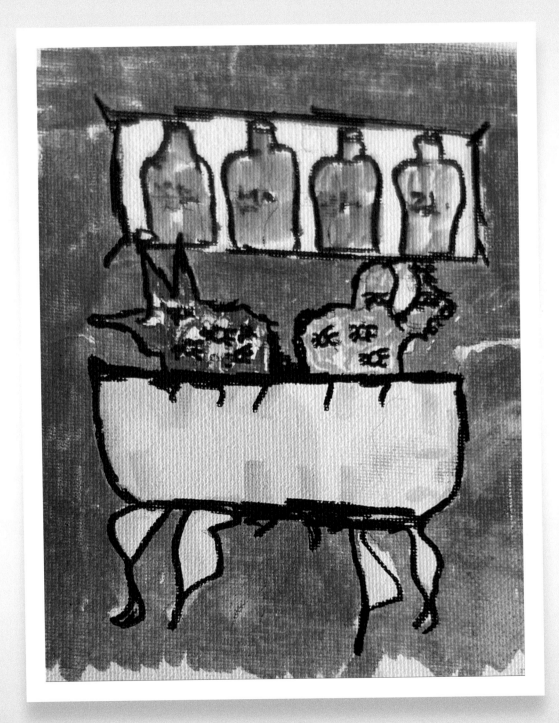

At one point in 2021 I looked for family in terms of nieces and nephews of theirs but didn't have much luck.

Shadow went to obedience school and was very adept at the dog obstacle course.

All dogs got regular massages from the Healing Arts by Margaret. They loved it.

Shadow always lived in one house. He is currently 11 years old and going strong.

Printed in the United States
by Baker & Taylor Publisher Services